The
Christmas Bunny

By Arnold Rabin
Illustrated by Carolyn Ewing

A GOLDEN BOOK • NEW YORK
Western Publishing Company, Inc., Racine, Wisconsin 53404

On the day before Christmas, Santa was awakened from his afternoon nap by a great hullabaloo at the front door.

He heard Mrs. Claus say, "I'm sorry, you can't see Santa now. He's asleep and he needs his rest. He must travel the world tonight!"

But whoever was making the noise would not go away.
Santa jumped out of bed and went to see who was there.
Just as he got to the door, he heard the visitor say, "I must
see Santa! I simply must!"

Then Santa saw who the visitor was.

"Easter Bunny!" Santa said with a laugh. "What are you doing at the North Pole?"

The Easter Bunny hopped past Santa into the living room. He seated himself in Santa's large rocking chair.

"I've made up my mind!" the bunny announced. "I want to give out Easter eggs on Christmas Eve. So I'm going with you tonight. I've decided completely! Absolutely! And positively!"

Santa was thunderstruck. "Who ever heard of giving out Easter eggs at Christmastime? And whatever made you decide to do that?"

The Easter Bunny popped out of the chair and began to hop around the room. In his excitement he hopped on top of the Christmas tree.

"What decided me?" he asked. "I decided me, of course! Why, I've spent the last two months making Christmas Easter eggs. No! Easter Christmas eggs! No! I mean Easter eggs to give out at Christmas! Let me show you one."

The bunny whipped out a Christmas Easter egg, or an Easter Christmas egg, from the pocket of his clean white jacket. What a wonder it was!

There were tiny Christmas trees painted on it, with
leaves that looked like bunny ears and Christmas lights
that looked like Easter eggs.

"Do you like it?" the Easter Bunny asked proudly.
"It's very nice," Santa answered. "But—"
"But! But! But what?" demanded the bunny.
"But no one would know what to think," Santa explained. "People wouldn't know whether it was Christmas or Easter! I'm sorry, but I really think it would be most confusing!"

"I knew you'd say no!" cried the bunny. "But you'll see! I'll fool you! Completely! Absolutely! And positively!"

Then the Easter Bunny took a giant hop out of the room and through the front door. In a fluff of his tail, he was gone.

And Santa went back to his bed to continue his nap.

At sunset that Christmas Eve, Mrs. Claus awakened Santa. He ate a hearty dinner, checked his lists, and hitched up the reindeer. Then he climbed into his sleigh and turned around for one last look behind him.

Suddenly Santa saw something strange sticking up in the middle of the presents.

And just as suddenly the something strange started to wiggle!
And then it wiggled again!
And Santa knew there was only one thing that wiggled like that—the Easter Bunny's ears!
Quietly he reached over the boxes and bows and tickled one ear.

"You caught me! All right, you caught me!" shouted the
Easter Bunny, springing up from his hiding place and
tossing on his Santa hat. "But it won't do any good. I'm
coming with you!"

Santa roared with laughter because the bunny looked so
funny sitting in the middle of the presents.

"Now, wait a minute," Santa said gently. "I like you very much. But I can't have you traveling with me on Christmas Eve!"

The Easter Bunny bounced out of the sleigh and into Santa's arms. He jumped so fast, Santa almost didn't catch him in time.

"Please, please, please let me come with you. I have all my eggs ready to deliver. I won't be any trouble at all."

Santa knew he couldn't take the Easter Bunny with him. Somehow he had to make his friend understand. Santa thought . . . and thought . . . and then he thought of a wonderful plan.

"All right. You can come," said Santa. "But only on one condition."

"Anything! What is it?" the bunny shouted for joy.

"At Eastertime," said Santa, "you've got to let me give out Christmas presents."

"What do you mean!?!?" the bunny said with a gasp. "Who ever heard of that! Imagine getting Christmas presents at Eastertime! Why, no one would know whether to open presents or hunt for Easter eggs! And how would people find any eggs with boxes and bows and wrapping paper all over the floor?

"Oh, NO! NO! NOO! That's quite impossible!" the
Easter Bunny continued. "Completely! Absolutely! And
positively IMPOSSIBLE!"

"But," said Santa, "what's fair is fair."

"Who told you that was fair?" said the bunny. "Easter is
Easter and Christmas is Christmas. Why would anyone
want to mix them up?"

"I don't know," said Santa, trying not to laugh.

"And besides," the bunny added, "think of yourself. If
you gave out Christmas presents all night, you'd be too
sleepy to hunt for your own Easter eggs."

"You're right, Bunny," said Santa. "And you must think
of yourself, too. If you're not home asleep on Christmas
Eve, you might not get your presents!"

"Dear, dear!" cried the Easter Bunny. "Why didn't you say that before? You're right! I'd better get home and to sleep. Completely! Absolutely! And positively to sleep!"

And he hopped into the air with a whirl that took him half the world around.

Late that night Santa reached the Easter Bunny's house. When he started to fill the Easter Bunny's stocking, he felt something peculiar down in the toe. It was round and hard. He reached in to pull it out.

There in his hand was a Christmas Easter egg. Attached to it was a small piece of paper that had some writing on it.

The note from the Easter Bunny said, "*Dear Santa, here is a Christmas present for you. I hope you like it. I'll be seeing you at Eastertime. Merry Christmas!*"